The Three Little Pigs

❧ Fairy Tale Treasury ❧

Adapted by
Jane Jerrard

Illustrated by
Susan Spellman

Publications International, Ltd.

There once were three little pigs who each decided to build himself a house.

The first pig met a man with a bundle of straw. The pig asked for some straw and built his house from it. Soon, a wolf came along and knocked on the door, saying, "Little pig, little pig, let me come in."

The pig answered, "Not by the hair of my chinny chin chin." So, that big bad wolf huffed and puffed until he blew the straw house down.

The second pig met a man with a load of sticks. The pig decided to make his house out of sticks.

Along came the wolf, knocking on the door and saying, "Little pig, little pig, let me come in."

But the second little pig answered, "Not by the hair of my chinny chin chin." So, the big bad wolf huffed and he puffed, and he blew the stick house down!

The third little pig met a man with a load of bricks. He asked for some bricks and built a sturdy little house. The wolf came knocking at his door, saying, "Little pig, little pig, let me come in."

"Not by the hair of my chinny chin chin."

The wolf huffed and he puffed, and he puffed and he huffed some more. But he could not blow down the brick house.

At last he gave up all his huffing and puffing and said, "Dear pig, come with me to Farmer Smith's turnip field. I happen to know it is full of nice, fat turnips. I will come for you at six o'clock tomorrow."

"All right," agreed the little pig. But he got up at five o'clock, went to Farmer Smith's, and gathered all the turnips he could carry. He was back home by six, when the wolf arrived.

The wolf was very angry to hear he had been tricked. But he did not show it. Instead, he said, "Friend pig, I know of an apple tree just up the hill. I will come for you at five o'clock tomorrow."

The little pig awoke at four o'clock and hurried off to pick his apples, hoping to return before the wolf came. But this time he had to climb a tree, and the wolf came along before he could climb down.

"Good morning, pig," said the wolf, licking his chops. "I am pleased to find you here. Tell me, are the apples very good?"

"Let me throw you one," answered the pig, and he threw it as far as he could. When the wolf ran to get it, the pig jumped down and trotted away home. There he made himself a delicious apple pie.

The next day the wolf was back.

"Charming pig, won't you come with me to the fair?" he asked. "I'll be here for you at three o'clock."

"Why, I love fairs!" said the pig.

The pig slipped out early and went to the fair himself. He had a fine time there, and bought a nice new barrel for his rainwater.

On his way home with his new barrel, the little pig saw the wolf coming to meet him. The pig climbed inside the barrel to hide, and it rolled right down the hill. The sight of it frightened the wolf so much that he turned and ran!

Later, the wolf came to the pig's house and told him of the strange sight. The little pig laughed and said it had only been a barrel—and that he himself had been in it!

The wolf did not like being laughed at. He climbed up on the roof and shouted down the chimney, "Little pig, little pig, I'm coming in!"

At this, the little pig hung a big pot of water over the fire. When the wolf came down the chimney, he fell right into the boiling water, and that was the end of the big bad wolf!